Roodica
the Rude
and the Chariot
Challenge

CATNIP BOOKS
Published by Catnip Publishing Ltd.
14 Greville Street
London EC1N 8SB

First published 2010
1 3 5 7 9 10 8 6 4 2

A CIP catalogue record for this book is available from the British Library

ISBN 978-1-846470-73-8

Printed in Poland

www.catnippublishing.co.uk

ROODICA THE RUDE
and the Chariot Challenge
MARGARET RYAN
Catnip

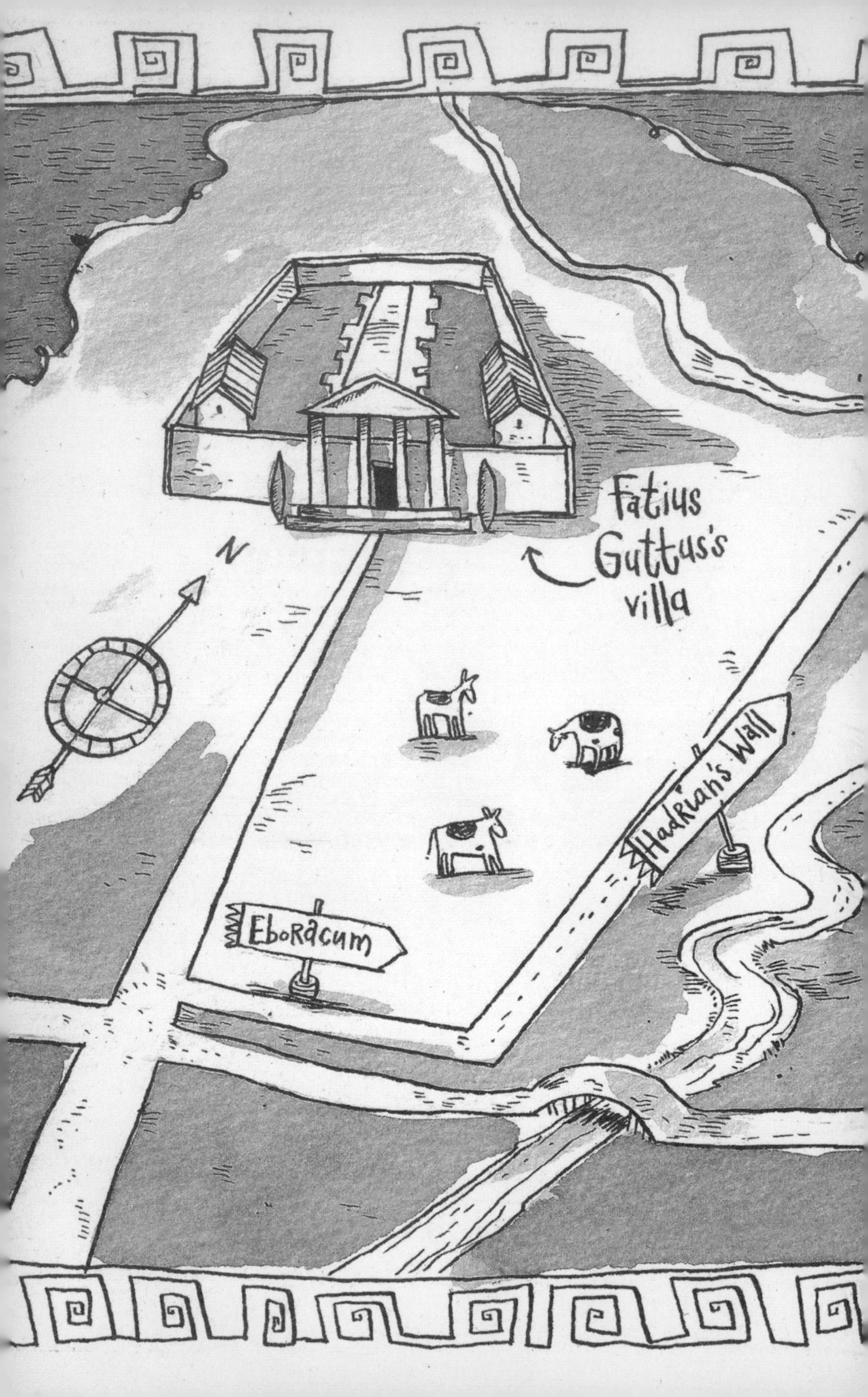
Fatius
Guttus's
villa
N
Hadrian's Wall
Eboracum

Madam Silverlock's cave
Maiden Castle
Sadler Sam's house
Will the Blacksmith's house
Gideon's house
Camulodunum
Watling Street
Verulamium

To Vasso, with love

Long, long, ago...

Back through the swirling mists of time when wolves and bears and wild boar roamed the land, and underpants hadn't been invented, the Romans thought it would be a 'superba idea' to invade Britain. The people of Britain, or Celts as they were then called, thought this was a rotten idea and fought back.

Thump! Thud! WALLOP! OUCH!

But despite that, the Romans won.

(Romans 1 - Celts 0)

And the Romans stayed. They built fine houses, straight roads and taught washing. "Don't forget to wash behind your ears, o stinkius peasant!"

They also collected taxes. Lots of taxes. King Bren of Brensland didn't like the taxes or the Romans. He preferred going off to war. So he did. Trouble was, he left his wife, Queen Goodica, and their three daughters, Foodica, Woodica and Roodica behind to fend for themselves…

Roodica's Royals (The Celts)

King of Brensland

Likes fighting, fighting and fighting. Oh, and wars, where he's usually to be found, right in the middle of the fighting.

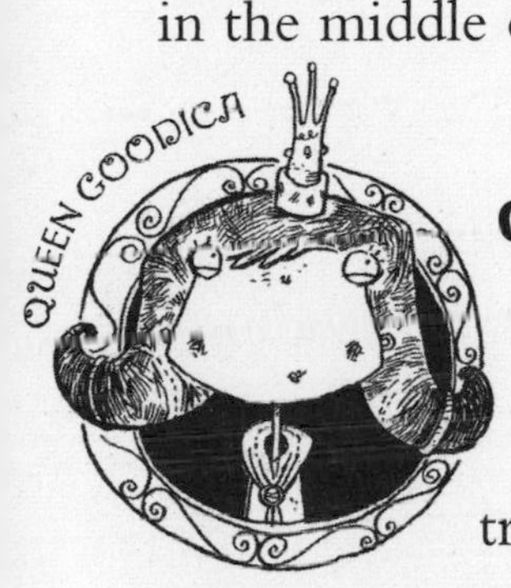

Queen of Brensland

Likes peace and quiet. Lives at Maiden Castle trying to bring up her three daughters as proper princesses.

Princess Foodica

The eldest daughter and a proper princess. She's always neat and tidy, never says anything wrong, and is a wonderful cook.

Princess Woodica

The middle daughter and a proper princess. She's always sweet and gentle, never does anything wrong, and makes wonderful things out of wood.

Princess Roodica

The youngest daughter and a proper…pain in the posterior. She's never neat and tidy, never sweet and gentle, and is always saying and doing everything wrong. Her mother wonders what on earth she'll do with her.

PRINCESS ROODICA

Roodica's Friends

Fleabag, the wolfhound

He goes everywhere
with Roodica.

Plodette, the pony

She carries Roodica
around sometimes.
Slowly.

Gideon, the horse boy

He tries to keep Roodica
out of trouble.
Fat chance!

The Terrible Togas (The Romans)

Magnus Maximus (Big Max)

Very superstitious Roman Governor. Likes ordering people about and getting presents. Wishes someone would hurry up and invent underpants as he finds Britain rather chilly.

Fatius Guttus (Fat Gut)

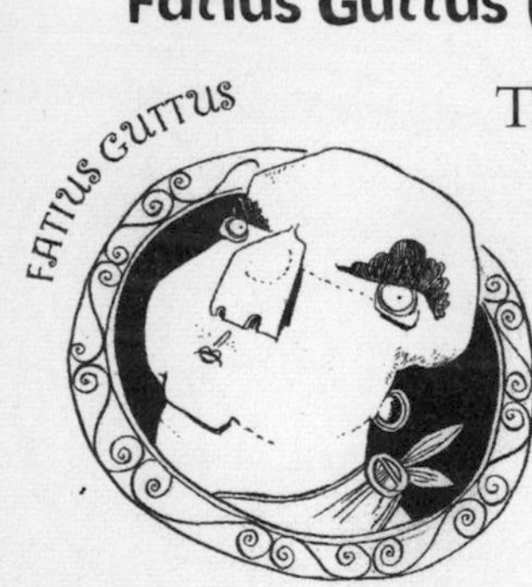

Tax Collector (Boo Hisssss). Likes collecting taxes, taxes, and more taxes, especially from those crummy Celts. Also likes eating, drinking and burping loudly.

Copius Mucus (Lottasnot)

Son of Fatius Guttus.

Likes telling tales,

sneaking up

on people

and sniffing.

Roodica Accepts the Challenge

It was lesson day again at Maiden Castle and Princess Roodica was glum.

"Why is the weather always fine on lesson days?" she asked Druid Big Brain, as she thumped herself down beside Gideon at the big table in the castle hall. "Why does it never rain? And why do lesson days come round more quickly than play days? Do you sneak in an extra one when I'm not looking?"

"You ask a lot of questions, Princess Roodica," smiled Druid Big Brain. But before he had a chance to answer them, there was the loud rumble of chariot wheels and the sound of horses' hooves. The door of Maiden Castle was flung open and Copius Mucus burst in.

"What are *you* doing here, Lottasnot?" demanded Roodica. "This is lesson day. Slimy Romans are not invited. Go away. Buzz off. **HOP it.**"

"Roodica, please don't be rude," said her mother, Queen Goodica. "Copius Mucus's tutor is unwell and Fatius Guttus has sent Copius to be educated here for a while."

Roodica scowled. "**HErE!** Why did no one tell me?"

"Because we knew you'd make a fuss," said Foodica.

"And probably yell a lot," said Woodica.

"ME, YELL?" yelled Roodica, as her mother and sisters left, holding their ears.

Copius smirked and sat down beside her. "I'm going to be so bored with these lessons since I'm much more intelligent than you are. Everyone knows the Celts are all as thick as Hadrian's Wall. However, Pater insists that I be here so… you may begin the lesson now," he instructed Druid Big Brain.

Druid Big Brain peered down his long nose at his three pupils. "Today I want you to talk about about your likes and dislikes. Gideon will begin."

Gideon thought for a moment. "I like Foodica's pancakes because they're buttery and delicious and melt in my mouth. I like training horses like Frisky because he's so clever he understands every word I say. And I like lesson days because they're interesting and I always learn something new."

"**SWOT,**" muttered Roodica, and kicked him under the table.

"**OW!** And I don't like people who kick me under the table."

Roodica tried to look innocent as Druid Big Brain gave her a hard stare.

"You're next, Princess Roodica," he said.

Roodica didn't have to think at all. "I like play days, my dog, Fleabag, and my horse, Plodette."

"That old nag," sneered Copius.

"And I don't like sneaky snots who come here to spy on us. A sick tutor. Huh!"

But Copius just smiled and said, "Now it's my turn. I like my new horse and the chariot my father has just given me. It's fast. It's fabulous. It's fantastic."

"It's a bore." Roodica gave a long yawn. "Who cares?"

Copius's smile turned nasty. "*You* might.

Pater bought it for me because there's to be a children's chariot race in town next market day, and I'm sure to win it *and* the big bag of prize money. No one else in this stupid country has a horse and chariot as fast as mine."

"Oh, you think so?" Roodica was annoyed. "I have a horse and chariot that are just as good as yours. Probably better."

"Rubbish," laughed Copius. "Your chariot's a heap of junk and your horse is a bag of bones. I've seen more meat on a butcher's apron."

"Children, children, we must get back to our lesson," said Druid Big Brain.

But no one was listening.

"I bet my horse and chariot could beat your horse and chariot any day," said Copius slyly.

"I bet they couldn't," said Roodica. "I bet my horse and chariot are the best."

"Then I challenge you to enter the chariot race and prove it."

"I will ***and*** I'll win the prize money," said Roodica.

"Fat chance," Copius smiled triumphantly. "I'll soon show you that we Romans are best at everything."

Gideon put his head in his hands and groaned. "You've done it now, Roodica. You haven't a hope against Copius."

"Don't worry, Giddy-up," whispered Roodica. "I think I know how to win the chariot challenge. I have a brilliant idea, but I need you to help me."

"That's why I'm worrying," said Gideon.

Will You Do Me a Favour?

When lesson day was over Copius climbed back into his fast, fabulous, fantastic chariot and whipped up his horse.

"See you at the starting line," he shouted to Roodica. "Bet you're still there when I'm collecting the prize money." And he drove off swiftly in a huge cloud of dust, which made Fleabag sneeze and dislodge several families of fleas.

Gideon shook his head gloomily.

"Copius is driving one of the new lightweight Roman chariots and his horse is a pure-bred Arab stallion. Your chariot's falling apart, Roodica, and Plodette is a pure-bred cart horse! You'll never be able to beat him."

"Nonsense," declared Roodica. "You're forgetting about my brilliant idea. Come on, we're going to see Will."

Roodica, Gideon and Fleabag headed down through the settlement to the blacksmith's. Will was by the fire, mending a hole in a cooking pot when they arrived.

"Hi, Will," said Roodica. "How are you?"

Will looked up. "I'm not doing it," he said.

"How do you know I want something? I haven't even asked you yet."

"I'm not doing it anyway. Whenever you want something it always means trouble."

"But I only want to really annoy Copius and win some prize money he's after for himself."

Will placed his iron back in the fire, put down the cooking pot, and scratched his head. "Annoy Copius? That's different. The little weasel's just come roaring past here in his fancy chariot and nearly took poor Lucky's leg off. Dog's only got three left as it is."

"Then you'll make me lighter tyres for my chariot by next week."

"What....!!!"

"Thanks, Will. I'll pay you back with the money I win," grinned Roodica, and hurried off before he could change his mind.

"Come on, Gideon. Come on, Fleabag, we'll go and see Sam next."

Fleabag's ears pricked up. He liked going to see the saddler.

Sam was outside his workshop polishing a saddle to a high gloss as they approached.

"Keep that horrible hound away from me, Roodica," he yelled.

But it was too late. With one bound Fleabag had toppled Sam over and was licking his face with his great wet tongue.

"If I tell him to leave you alone, will you do me a favour?" grinned Roodica.

There was a muffled grunt.

"I need to really annoy Copius and win some prize money he wants for himself. Could you make me a lightweight harness for Plodette by next week?"

There was a muffled explosion.

"Thanks, Sam. I'll pay you back with the money I win. Leave, Fleabag. Sam's face is clean enough now," grinned Roodica, and hurried off before Sam could change his mind.

"Now all we need to do is make my chariot lighter," she said to Gideon.

"That's easy," he said. "You only need to look at it and bits fall off."

But Roodica just laughed. "Come on, we've got a lot of work to do and we haven't got much time."

The Old Chariot

Roodica, Gideon and Fleabag hurried back up the hill to Maiden Castle. The old chariot was in its usual place beside the front door and, as always, it was filled with ducks.

They squawked loudly when Roodica carefully lifted them out. "Sorry guys, but you'll need to find somewhere else to snooze for a while. We need the old chariot."

The ducks waddled off huffily towards the nearest barn and Roodica grabbed the chariot by the long front pole.

"Help me move this round the back of the castle to Plodette's field," she said to Gideon. "We can work on it there out of sight. I don't want the queen and my sisters to find out what I'm doing."

The two of them hauled the creaky,

rumbly old chariot away, but the noise soon attracted the attention of the settlement children who came running to see what was happening.

"What are you doing, Roodica?" they asked.

Roodica turned and let the chariot pole drop. It fell on Gideon's big toe.

She put her finger to her lips. "Can you keep a secret ?" she whispered to the children, as Gideon hopped about on one foot.

"Of course."

"We're going to fix up the old chariot, so I can beat Copius in the children's chariot race on market day," she said.

"Great idea," the children whispered back. "He nearly ran us over in his stupid, new chariot. Can we help?"

"You could take it in turns to ride Plodette up and down the field," said Roodica. "She'll need a lot more exercise if she's to be ready for the race."

"No problem," said the children, and raced to be first to reach the piebald pony.

"Now," Roodica turned to Gideon, who was still hopping. "I'll slip into the castle and get a broom to clean out the chariot while you decide which bits we can do without."

Gideon shook his head. "This'll never work," he said. "You're crazy, loopy, seriously bonkers to even ***think*** it will."

But Roodica had already hurried off and wasn't listening.

Roodica came back with the broom and Gideon stood well clear as she swept duck poo up into the air. When the chariot was cleaned out, she helped Gideon saw several thick pieces of wood from the sides.

"We still need these bits, but I'll smooth them down and make them as thin as I can," said Gideon. "Just don't lean on them while you're driving."

"What about the wheels?" said Roodica, giving them a kick. "They're really thick and clunky and one of them's got a broken spoke."

"And they're really wobbly," muttered Gideon. "I'll take them off and make narrower ones. Then Will can fit his lighter, iron tyres to the new ones."

"I'll help you take off the wheels," said Roodica. "This is much better than lessons."

"Okay," said Gideon, and bent down and removed two long pieces of iron which he handed to Roodica.

"They're really heavy," she said. "The chariot will be a lot lighter without them."

Gideon sighed. "Don't you know

anything? These are the lynch pins. They drop into a hole in the axle and stop the wheels falling off. I hope," he added, shaking his head.

"You worry too much. It'll be fine," said Roodica.

"No, it won't. The chariot will fall apart at the first bump."

"I'll drive carefully," said Roodica.

Gideon snorted in disbelief.

"There's also the small matter of Plodette," he said, as the pony wandered past with a little boy on her back.

"She couldn't run fast if her tail were on fire."

"You're wrong," grinned Roodica. "I've seen her run really fast, and that's where you come in. You and Frisky. You're part of my brilliant idea. Now all I have to do is persuade the queen to go into town on market day so I can take part in the chariot race...."

Going to Town

Queen Goodica wasn't keen to go into town on market day.

"I don't really like the town on market day," she said, looking up from her sewing. "It's always so noisy and messy and smelly."

"Just hitch your skirt up over your knees and jump over the cowpats. That's what I do," said Roodica.

The queen shuddered. "Roodica, do try

to remember you're a princess. I don't think jumping over..."

"Well, it's better than getting poo on your shoe because then your feet are pongy all day, and the flies come after you and dive bomb your toes and..."

"THAT'S QUITE ENOUGH ROODICA!" said her mother. "I don't know where you get these ideas from..."

"Actually, I'd *like* to go to the town on market day," said Foodica.

"I love looking at all the different food stalls and, if I made a lot of pancakes, perhaps Gideon could sell some for me."

Roodica frowned. "Gideon will be busy. Why can't you sell them yourself?"

"Because princesses don't sell things at market stalls."

Roodica made her exploding duck noise.

"I'd like to go to the market too," said Woodica. "I love listening to the wandering bards playing their harps and singing

about the old battles at Verulamium and Camulodunum, though sadly we lost both of them. And I've made a lot of wooden beads, perhaps Gideon could sell some of them for me."

"**Didn't you hear me, cloth ears?** Why don't you listen instead of wittering on about wooden beads and old battles. I **said** Gideon would be busy," yelled Roodica.

"Princesses don't sell and princesses don't yell, Roodica," said the queen sternly. "Why are you so keen to go into town anyway?"

Roodica calmed down and thought for a moment. If princesses didn't sell and princesses didn't yell, they probably didn't race chariots either.

"I… er… told Copius I'd watch out for him in the children's chariot race," she said, crossing her fingers behind her back.

"I see," the queen smiled. "I'm really glad you're getting on better with Copius. I know his father lied about his tutor being unwell. I know he really sent him here to keep an eye on us, but there's no point in upsetting the Romans if we can avoid it… We'll go into town on market day."

"**Hooray,**" cried Roodica and jumped up and down.

"Gideon can drive us."

Roodica stopped jumping. "Er… no, Gideon will be busy."

"Gideon is very busy all of a sudden. What exactly is he busy doing?"

"Oh, this and that," said Roodica, studying her fingernails. "One thing and another… bits and bobs..."

"Then who will take us?" asked the queen.

"Why me, of course," said Roodica.

"You!" exclaimed her mother and sisters in alarm. "We'll never get to town alive."

"We will," promised Roodica. "I'll drive very slowly and carefully." And added under her breath, "I'll have to. It's the only way I'll get the old chariot there in one piece."

The New Improved Chariot

Two days before the chariot challenge, Roodica and Gideon rolled the narrower, wooden wheels Gideon had made down the hill to the blacksmith's.

"Oh, there you arc," grunted Will. "The new tyres are ready. I've made them as light as I can."

"Thank you, Will. They look great," said Roodica, and watched while he clamped them into place around the wooden wheels. Then she and Gideon rolled the wheels back up the hill to Plodette's field and fitted them onto the chariot.

"Now, don't forget to hammer the lynch pins in carefully, Gideon." Roodica grinned. "We don't want the wheels to fall off during the race, do we?"

Gideon scowled. He finished fixing the wheels, then Roodica helped him replace the chariot's new wooden sides.

"You've worked really hard on them, Gideon," said Roodica, running her fingers along the silky wood. "How did you get them so smooth?"

"Hard work and coarse sand," said Gideon.

"Well, the old chariot looks fantastic.

Thank you," said Roodica, and left Fleabag with Gideon while she slipped down to saddler Sam's to collect Plodette's new harness.

"Glad to see you're on your own," growled Sam. "The new harness is ready. I've made it as light as I can."

"Thank you, Sam. It looks great."

Roodica carried the harness back to Maiden Castle hidden under a coarse woollen blanket.

"What have you got there, Roodica?" asked the settlement children.

Roodica looked about to make sure no one else was looking, then gathered them round her. "Can you keep another secret?" she asked.

"Of course."

"This is Plodette's new harness for the race," she whispered. "But I don't want the queen to see it. She still doesn't know about the chariot challenge."

"We won't tell," the children whispered back. "But on market day we'll all come into town to cheer you on."

"Good," smiled Roodica, and slipped into the castle and hid the harness in the old blanket chest.

At last market day arrived. Roodica got up early, collected the harness and sneaked out of Maiden Castle to groom Plodette. She combed her mane and her tail and brushed her flanks till they shone. Plodette took no notice, but Fleabag did. He watched from a safe distance in case Roodica decided to smarten him up too. After a while Gideon appeared leading Frisky. He had a bag of pancakes and a bag of beads hung from his saddle. Plodette neighed in pleasure at seeing the other horse and nuzzled him gently. While

she was busy, Gideon and Roodica polished her hooves.

"I still think this is a crazy idea," said Gideon. "You'll never beat Copius and everyone will laugh at you. Then the queen will be angry and I'll get the blame for letting you do stupid things."

"Rubbish. Just be at the finishing line with Frisky when the race starts. And don't worry about selling the pancakes or the beads. Nothing must get in the way of my brilliant idea..."

Later, however, when the queen and her elder daughters came out of Maiden Castle and saw the chariot, they didn't

think riding in it was such a brilliant idea.

"Plodette looks very smart in that new harness," admitted the queen, "but what happened to the old chariot? It looks a lot smarter too, but there doesn't seem to be as much of it as before."

"It's the new streamlined, lightweight look Gideon and I have been working

on," said Roodica. "It's very fashionable."

"It doesn't look very safe," said Foodica.

"Or very comfortable," said Woodica.

"Oh, stop moaning and just get in," muttered Roodica. "Not you, Fleabag. There isn't room. You'll have to run alongside."

Roodica climbed in after her mother

and sisters and took up the reins.

"Now drive carefully," warned her mother.

"Don't worry. I will," said Roodica.

And to the queen's surprise, she did. She didn't rattle everyone's teeth by bumping over tree roots. She didn't take corners on one wheel. She didn't even soak everyone by deliberately splattering through the muddiest puddles, and they all arrived safely in town.

"That was a very pleasant journey, Roodica," said the queen. "I'm glad to see you are learning sense at last."

Roodica smiled but said nothing.

"Now let's stroll through the market. I'd

like to look at the Indian silks, though we can't afford to buy any," sighed the queen.

"I'd like to see if Gideon's managed to sell any of my pancakes," said Foodica.

"Or any of my beads," said Woodica.

"You three go ahead," said Roodica. "I'll just…er…find a good place to park the chariot."

The Big Race

Roodica drove a little way to the field at the edge of the market. It was crowded with townspeople waiting for the chariot race to begin. Up on a specially built platform sat the Roman dignitaries. Roodica recognised the governor, Magnus Maximus and the tax collector, Fatius Guttus.

"Couldn't mistake *him*," she muttered to Fleabag, who was runnning alongside.

"Not with a belly that size. Looks like he swallowed an ox."

Then she found a place to park the chariot. Right on the starting line for the race. Right beside Copius.

As she lined up, she gazed at him in amazement. Copius was wearing a

leather helmet, knee-pads and shin-pads. A broad gold border on his white tunic matched the gleaming metal on his chariot, while his horse's harness jingled with gold bells. The stallion's tail had been neatly pleated and threaded with tiny pearls.

"What...!"

Copius laughed when he saw Roodica's face. "I see you've dressed up for the occasion," he sneered. "Where did you get your tunic? From the local tramp? Huh, some princess. A chariot made out of firewood and a horse that can hardly stand. What a joke. She'll probably drop dead before the race starts."

"Why don't you drop dead, Slimeboy!"

But Copius simply laughed. "Just watch me collect the prize money," he said.

"I see you have some competition, Copius," called his father, Fatius Guttus, from the platform, laughing and pointing at Roodica. "Good luck."

"Won't need it," smirked Copius, as he picked up his whip ready for the start.

Roodica patted Plodette's flank.

"Do your very best," she said.

"Plodette, Plodette. She's the fastest pony yet,"

chanted some small voices from nearby.

Roodica looked round and waved to the settlement children. "Stay with the children," she ordered Fleabag. "I don't want you getting squashed under Copius's wheels."

Fleabag shook off some fleas and sloped off.

A moment later, Plodette gave a great snort as a volley of trumpets sounded and Magnus Maximus stood up. He adjusted his laurel wreath and waved regally to the crowd. The race was about to begin. Then the Roman governor lifted his hand, dropped a white hanky, and they were off.

Copius's horse immediately took the lead while the others in the race jostled for

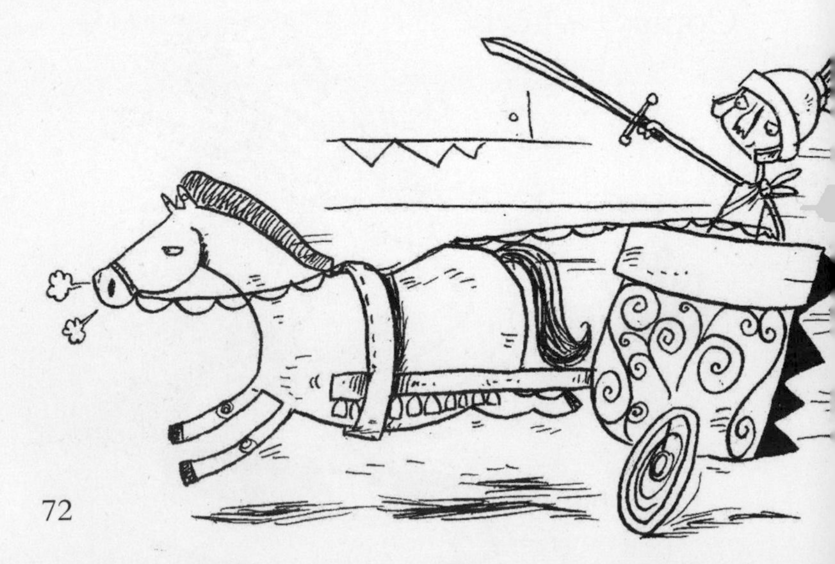

position behind him. Plodette brought up the rear.

"COME ON, PLODETTE,"

yelled Roodica, jumping up and down and flicking the reins. "There's a bucket of oats waiting for you back home. You can go faster than that!"

Plodette tried a bit harder, but she was still last.

Copius was still leading the field.

"Vade! Vade! Go! Go!"

he screamed, cracking his whip.

"Come on, Plodette,"

yelled Roodica. "I'll buy you a bucket of carrots if you go faster."

Plodette tried even harder, but she was still last.

By now Copius was waving triumphantly to the crowd and whipping his horse towards the finishing line.

"Come on, Plodette," yelled Roodica. "You can't let that crummy little creep beat you. What would Frisky say? He's at the finishing line waiting for you."

Plodette looked up and saw Frisky. That did it. With a tremendous effort, she picked up her big hooves and thundered down the field. Bits of the chariot's side flew off as she skidded and dodged past all the others and caught up with Copius.

Then she blew out her nostrils, stretched her great neck, and just pipped his Arab stallion at the post.

"And it's Plodette by a nose," declared the amazed judge. "Princess Roodica wins the children's chariot race!"

Copius couldn't believe it.

"Yyyyou," he stuttered, his face like thunder. "It's not possible. How did you do it?"

"Sheer brilliance," gasped Roodica, as Plodette stopped abruptly beside Frisky and nearly catapulted her from the chariot into the cheering crowd.

"Well done, Plodette," smiled Gideon, patting her steaming flank. "Well done, Roodica. I didn't think you'd win."

"Win what?" asked Queen Goodica, moving swiftly through the crowd.

"Er…there was a children's chariot race and I just won it and lots of prize money," said Roodica. "I know princesses don't sell or yell or race chariots but…"

"On the contrary," smiled the queen. "You are related to the great queen Boudicca and she was an excellent charioteer."

The crowd cheered again and Foodica and Woodica gave Roodica a hug. They didn't even scold her when she told them Gideon had been too busy looking after Frisky to sell the pancakes or the wooden beads.

"We can eat the pancakes on the way home," grinned Roodica, "and keep the beads to wear with our new tunics, now we can afford to buy the Indian silk. Then I must pay Will and Sam for the new wheels and the harness, and buy carrots for Frisky and Plodette."

"You've done really well, Roodica," smiled her mother.

"I knew Plodette would run like mad to get to Frisky," grinned Roodica, "and the prize money's great, but best of all, I really, really enjoyed annoying that snivelling, snotty, horrible little slimy slug, Copius."

"Princesses may race chariots, but they don't call people names, Roodica," said the queen.

Roodica crossed her fingers behind her back. "I'll try to remember that," she said.